PUFFIN BOOKS

Tumbleweed

Dick King-Smith served in the Grenadier Guards during the Second World War, and afterwards spent twenty years as a farmer in Gloucestershire, the county of his birth. Many of his stories are inspired by his farming experiences. Later he taught at a village primary school. His first book, *The Fox Busters,* was published in 1978. Since then he has written a great number of children's books, including *The Sheep-Pig* (winner of the *Guardian* Award and filmed as *Babe*), *Harry's Mad, Noah's Brother, The Hodgeheg, Martin's Mice, Ace, The Cuckoo Child* and *Harriet's Hare* (winner of the Children's Book Award in 1995). At the British Book Awards in 1992 he was voted Children's Author of the Year. He is married, with three children and eleven grandchildren, and lives in a seventeenth-century cottage a short crow's-flight from the house where he was born.

D0806401

DICK KING-SMITH

TUMBLEWEED

Illustrated by Harry Horse

PUFFIN BOOKS

PUFFIN BOOKS

Published by the Penguin Group
Penguin Books Ltd, 27 Wrights Lane, London W8 5TZ, England
Penguin Putnam Inc., 375 Hudson Street, New York, New York 10014, USA
Penguin Books Australia Ltd, Ringwood, Victoria, Australia
Penguin Books Canada Ltd, 10 Alcorn Avenue, Toronto, Ontario, Canada M4V 3B2
Penguin Books (NZ) Ltd, Private Bag 102902, NSMC, Auckland, New Zealand

Penguin Books Ltd, Registered Offices: Harmondsworth, Middlesex, England

First published by Victor Gollancz 1987
Published in Puffin Books 1988
This edition with new illustrations published in Puffin Books 1999
3 5 7 9 10 8 6 4 2

Typeset in Baskerville

Made and printed in England by Clays Ltd, St Ives plc

British Library Cataloguing in Publication Data
A CIP catalogue record for this book is available from the British Library

ISBN 0-141-30238-0

CHAPTER 1

The stillness of the forest glade was broken by a sudden noise.

It sounded like someone crying 'Help!' from inside a tin can, and in a way that's what it was. Sir Tumbleweed was in trouble again.

Sir Tumbleweed was a tall thin knight, with bright red hair and a long red moustache that drooped sadly at either end. Of all the knights in Merrie England, he was the most accident-prone. He was also a very nervous man. For instance, he was scared of horses. They were so large (they had to be, to carry knights in heavy armour) that once he was mounted (hoisted aboard by block and tackle) he seemed to be a

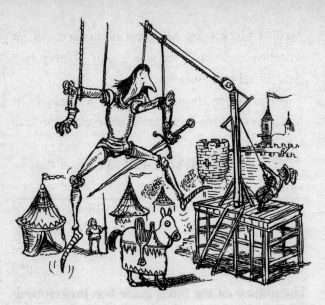

frighteningly long way from the ground. Being scared of heights, Sir Tumbleweed would throw his armoured arms around the animal's neck. Off would go the startled horse, and off would come Sir Tumbleweed. Once down, he could not get up, and many a lonely hour he spent lying on the ground shouting 'Help!' inside his helmet.

This time he was luckier. At the third 'Help!' precisely, he looked up to see a figure bending over him. It was dressed all in black. It wore a tall black hat upon its head, and a long black cloak, against whose hem a black cat rubbed

2

itself. A black scarf hid most of its face. All Sir Tumbleweed could see was a pair of grey eyes that stared into his own.

A witch! he thought, and knew, though he had never before met one, that he was scared of witches.

Sir Tumbleweed lay rigid, convinced that he would be turned into a frog.

I might be better off as a frog, he thought. At least I wouldn't have to wear this horrible armour, or ride that horrible horse, or do any of the other things I'm supposed to do, like jousting or killing dragons or rescuing damsels in distress. Go on then, he thought, see if I care.

'Relax,' said the witch. 'I won't.'

Curiously, for Sir Tumbleweed had no doubt that she was hideously ugly, her voice, instead of being a harsh cackle, was low and pleasant.

'Won't what?' he said.

'Turn you into a frog.'

'You read my mind!' gasped Sir Tumbleweed.

'It's just one of the things that hideously ugly witches can do.'

Sir Tumbleweed blushed.

'I suppose you know my name?'

'Yes, Sir Tumbleweed.'

'And you know I've never rescued a damsel, or tackled a dragon because I'm too nervous, and never had a tilt at another knight because I always fall off before I get there?'

'Yes,' said the witch. 'I know all those things. And I know you need help. Because you said so. Why don't you start by helping yourself?'

'How?'

'First, take off your helmet.'

After a struggle, during which his visor snapped shut and nearly took his nose off, Sir Tumbleweed removed his helmet.

'Phew!' he said. 'That's a weight off my mind.'

'Now your gauntlets.'

He peeled off his armour-plated gloves.

'And your hauberk.'

Off came his chain mail coat.

'And now your cuirass and your greaves.'

Obediently Sir Tumbleweed undid his heavy breastplate and his leg-armour.

'Now then,' said the witch, 'oops-a-daisy,' and lightly Sir Tumbleweed sprang to his feet and stood before her in tunic and hose.

'There!' said the witch. 'Does that feel better?'

'Oh yes, thanks!' cried Sir Tumbleweed. And he ran trippingly towards his charger which was grazing close by. He put his foot in the stirrup and swung himself up into the saddle with such abandon that he fell off the other side. The horse galloped away.

'Let it go,' said the witch. 'A clumsy great beast like that is no use to you.'

'But if I haven't got a horse,' said Sir Tumbleweed, 'and I haven't any armour on, how can I be a brave knight?'

'How can you be a brave knight anyway?' said the witch gently.

Sir Tumbleweed sighed. The ends of his red moustache seemed to droop even further.

'You're right,' he said gloomily. 'I'm not brave. In fact I'm scared of most things.'

He stared uncomfortably into those grey eyes, which still were all he could see of the witch's face.

'But of course you knew that already,' he said.

'Let me ask you something,' said the witch. 'Do you think that to be brave means to be fearless?'

'Yes.'

'You are wrong, Sir Tumbleweed. To be truly brave is to know fear and yet to overcome it. Now suppose you had to face a lion. What would you feel?'

'Terrified,' said Sir Tumbleweed.

'What would you do?'

'Run like billy-o,' said Sir Tumbleweed. He shivered. 'Thank goodness there aren't any lions in these parts,' he said. 'The very mention of one puts the wind up me. I prefer cats the size yours is.'

He bent down to stroke the witch's cat, but, as he did so, its ears went flat, its mouth opened in a soundless snarl, its back curved into a hoop and it stuck its fluffed-out tail straight up in the air.

Sir Tumbleweed drew back nervously. Then he saw that the cat was not looking at him. It was looking past him. It was looking at something just behind him.

An icy shiver ran down Sir Tumbleweed's long spine. He turned, and found himself facing a very large lion.

CHAPTER 2

Sir Tumbleweed's heart stood still. So did the lion. Only his tongue moved as thoughtfully he licked his chops.

Slowly, very slowly, the knight took a step back. And another step. Then he felt a hard little hand in the small of his back and heard that low gentle voice in his ear.

'It's no use running away,' whispered the witch. 'He's much too close. You must stand your ground and stare him out. Now's your chance to prove yourself a brave knight. After all, he's only a brute beast.'

'He's a hell of a big beast,' muttered Sir Tumbleweed miserably. 'Couldn't you turn him into a frog? I could stare a frog out.'

At that moment the lion took a step forward and opened his jaws very wide, showing an array of razor-sharp teeth.

'AAAAAAARRRRRGGGGGHHHHH!!' he roared.

'AAAAAAARRRRRGGGGGHHHHH!!' yelled Sir Tumbleweed in terror. At the sound of this yell the lion stopped and an anxious look came over his face.

'You've got him worried,' whispered the witch. 'Do it again.'

'AAAAAAARRRRRGGGGGHHHHH!!' yelled the horrified knight once more. This time the lion took a step backwards.

'Now,' said the witch, 'see him off!' And she gave Sir Tumbleweed a hefty push.

Caught off balance, he tripped over his feet and almost fell. He waved his arms madly in an effort to stay upright and, at the sight of this strange tall figure cartwheeling wildly towards him, the lion turned and fled with his tail between his legs.

'I thought you said,' remarked the witch slowly, 'that you were scared of most things?'

'I am, I am!' said Sir Tumbleweed, mopping his brow.

'But not, apparently, of lions. You told me you would run like billy-o if you met one. Yet now look what happens. Not only did you stand and face the beast – you actually charged at it!'

'But . . .' began Sir Tumbleweed.

'No buts,' said the witch. 'We saw you, didn't we, Grim?'

The black cat purred loudly and rubbed itself against the knight's legs.

'We saw you, an unarmed man, put a full-grown lion to flight!'

'Well, you see . . .' began Sir Tumbleweed.

'I see all right,' said the witch. 'I see before me not just a knight, not just a bold knight, but the boldest knight in Merrie England.'

'You do?'

'Certainly I do. No one else could have done what you did.'

'They couldn't?'

'Such coolness in the face of danger! Such ferocity in that great battlecry you gave! Such speed and resolution in attack! I've never known anything like it.'

'You haven't?'

'Never. Despite the fact that you knew fear . . .'

'Oh yes, not half!'

'. . . yet you overcame it.'

'I did?' said Sir Tumbleweed.

His face, which had been deathly white, turned pink with pleasure. His hands stopped shaking. His teeth stopped chattering. Even the ends of his moustache seemed to rise, in keeping with his spirits.

'I did!' he said. 'I did!'

He puffed out his narrow chest.

'D'you know,' he said, 'I feel so good, I almost

wish that brute would come back. I'd show it who was master!'

'I'm awfully sorry,' said a deep rumbly voice.

Sir Tumbleweed spun round to see that the lion had indeed returned, and was lying close by with his head on his crossed forepaws and a most apologetic look upon his face.

'I shouldn't have roared at you,' said the lion. 'It was very rude of me, I'm afraid.'

'You're afraid! I should jolly well think you were afraid!' said Sir Tumbleweed. 'I soon scared you, didn't I?'

'You certainly did,' said the lion.

'I showed you who was master!'

'You did,' said the lion humbly. 'Master.'

'He's taken a fancy to you,' said the witch.

'What!' cried Sir Tumbleweed. 'Oh, I see what you mean. Well, he's not a bad animal, is he?'

'Perhaps you could keep him for a pet,' said the witch.

'I say, that's an idea! I mean, other people would be scared of him even if I'm not.'

He turned to the lion.

'Come here, boy,' he said.

'Yes, master,' said the lion, crawling closer.

'What's your name?' asked Sir Tumbleweed.

'Arthur,' said the lion. 'If you please, master.'

'Good boy, Arthur,' said Sir Tumbleweed, and he patted the top of his new pet's enormous hairy head.

'You aren't going to need that old suit of armour of yours any more,' said the witch. 'Not while he's around. But we don't want to leave rubbish about, messing up the countryside, so perhaps you'd better go and pick it up.'

She waited until Sir Tumbleweed was out of earshot, and then she said softly, 'Nice work, Arthur.'

'What a performance, Art!' purred the black cat, Grim. '"Yes master", "No master", "Three bags full master" – honestly, it's enough to make a cat laugh!'

'I didn't overdo it, did I?' asked the lion anxiously.

'No,' said the witch, stroking his ears. 'It was just right. Thanks to you, that nervous knight now considers himself braver than a lion.'

CHAPTER 3

Sir Tumbleweed came staggering back with his arms full of armour, and dropped it with a crash.

'Phew!' he said. 'Weighs a ton, that lot. You freeze inside it in the winter and in summer you sweat buckets. What are we going to do with it?'

'Shut your eyes and count to ten,' said the witch, and when the knight reopened them, it was to find that almost all his knightly panoply had vanished. Only his sword remained. All the rest – helmet, gauntlets, hauberk, cuirass, greaves – were gone.

'Thought I'd better leave you your sword,'

the witch said. 'It was a bit blunt, so I've put a decent edge on it for you. Give it a try.'

'What on?' said Sir Tumbleweed.

'Oh, that tree over there,' she said, pointing to a fine young oak with a trunk a foot thick.

'You must be joking!' giggled Sir Tumbleweed, but just for fun he whirled the sword around his head and struck at the tree with all his strength (which wasn't much).

To his amazement, the blade sliced through the oak like a knife through butter, and down it came with an almighty crash.

'Well I never did!' said Sir Tumbleweed.

'It seems you're as strong as a lion too,' said the witch. 'Why, there isn't a knight in all the land that you couldn't slay.'

Sir Tumbleweed looked worried.

'I'm not mad about slaying people,' he said doubtfully, 'but I'll tell you what I've always fancied, shall I?'

'What's that?' said Grim.

'Tell us, master,' said Arthur.

'I've always fancied winning a Tournament. You know, tipping all the other chaps off their horses, one after another. It looks such fun, but like I said, I've always fallen off before I ever got

a tilt at anybody. Anyway, now I haven't got a horse or a lance.'

'What else would you like to do?' asked the witch. 'Kill a dragon? You could use your sword for that.'

'One good swipe . . .' mewed Grim.

'And off comes his head!' roared Arthur.

'That might be fun,' said Sir Tumbleweed. 'Specially if the dragon had taken a prisoner.'

'What sort of a prisoner?' said the witch.

Sir Tumbleweed looked rather coy.

'A damsel,' he said. 'In distress.'

Between the brim of her black hat and the

rim of her black scarf, the witch's grey eyes twinkled.

'You'd like to rescue a damsel, would you?' she said.

'Oh, rather!' said Sir Tumbleweed.

'Bit of a lady's man, are you?'

The knight blushed.

'Oh, I don't know about that,' he said. 'I mean, I like girls, but they always seem to go for the big beefy chaps.'

'What sort of damsel would you fancy?' asked the witch.

Sir Tumbleweed pulled the ends of his red moustache thoughtfully.

'She'd have to be tall, I think,' he said, 'because I'm such a long stick, you see. I'd look a bit silly with a very short girl.'

'How tall?'

'Oh, about your height,' said Sir Tumbleweed, 'and with eyes the same colour as yours,' he added gallantly. But she'd have to be jolly pretty, he thought before he could stop himself thinking it.

'And, of course, she would be beautiful,' said the witch, and there seemed to be something in the tone of that strangely pleasant voice that made Sir Tumbleweed feel suddenly very sorry for her.

'Oh, I don't know,' he said. 'It's much more important to be nice, than to be pretty. I mean – you're nice.'

'Thanks,' said the witch drily. 'And what would you do when you'd rescued this tall, grey-eyed, pretty, nice damsel?'

'Why, marry her of course,' said Sir Tumbleweed, 'and live happily ever after.' He pulled his moustache again, frowning.

'If she'd have me, that is,' he said. 'I'm no oil painting.'

'But you're brave, master,' said Arthur.

'I am, aren't I!'

'And you'll soon chop a dragon up with that sword,' said Grim.

'I will, won't I!'

'And if you entered a Tournament,' said the witch, 'and defeated all comers and became the Champion, she wouldn't be able to resist you.'

'She wouldn't, would she!' said Sir Tumbleweed delightedly.

Then his face fell.

'Trouble is,' he said, 'I'm such a rotten horseman. I mean, I'll probably be better

without all that ironmongery, but these chargers are such huge great beasts. I always feel I'd be much happier on a little horse, where I could put my feet down either side if I needed to.'

'That might be arranged,' said the witch.

'And those lances – they're so long and clumsy. I always feel a little one would be better. If you caught them right, I'm sure you could tip chaps off with a little one.'

'That might be arranged,' said the witch.

'I bet I could run rings round the other fellows if I had a little horse and a little lance,' said Sir Tumbleweed.

'A little horse and a little lance,' repeated the witch thoughtfully. She turned to the lion. 'Does that ring a bell with you, Arthur?' she said, and she winked the grey eye furthest from Sir Tumbleweed.

'Eh?' said the lion.

'Oh,' he said.

'Ah, I get you,' he said. 'You mean a . . .!'

'I mean', said the witch quickly, 'that I must be off because I've a lot of spells to cast, and anyway Grim needs his supper. Sir Tumbleweed, why don't you take Arthur for a little walk in the forest?'

'Good thinking,' said the knight. 'Need to stretch the old legs. Come, Arthur!'

'Yes, master,' said the lion.

'And walk to heel, there's a good boy.'

'After all,' he shouted back to the witch, 'you never know what we might find, do you?'

'Me?' said the witch. 'How could I?'

CHAPTER 4

Knight and lion walked companionably
through the forest. Sir Tumbleweed strode out
on long thin legs while at his heel Arthur, heavy
head swinging, paced silently along with the
slouching, rolling, powerful gait of his kind.

Sir Tumbleweed felt very light-hearted.
Walking was so enjoyable without the weight of
all that armour and if, as often happened, he
should trip over a tree-root or slip upon a slidy
slope, he could steady himself by grasping
Arthur's shaggy mane. And what other knight
had his own lion! Nothing to fear with Arthur
around and with so sharp a sword in hand.
Nothing to fear anyway, he thought, because

now I am fearless, and then he jumped a mile as a bird burst suddenly from a bush with a shriek of alarm.

'What is the matter, master?' said the lion.

'Not a thing,' said Sir Tumbleweed. 'Just practising jumping,' and he leaped in the air several times in an experimental way.

'A chap has to keep fit, you know,' he said, and he drew his sword and began to cut and thrust madly at imaginary foes.

'On guard!' he shouted, and 'Have at you!' and 'Take that, base varlet!' Until finally he took

a tremendous swipe at a nearby sapling, and missed and fell flat on his face.

As Sir Tumbleweed began to lever himself up from the ground, he saw a number of marks in the soft mould on the forest floor, and very familiar marks they were to a man who had spent his life falling off horses.

'Look, Arthur!' he said. 'Hoofprints! And little ones too. Little hooves, little horse.'

'No doubt of it, master,' said Arthur. He dropped his great head and snuffled at them.

'Fresh, too,' he said. 'Perhaps we should follow them? The animal must be riderless, for the prints are not deep. A forest pony maybe – that would be just what we need.'

'But how shall we catch it?'

'Leave that to me, master.'

A nasty thought crossed Sir Tumbleweed's mind.

'I say, Arthur,' he said. 'No rough stuff, mind. This creature's for me to ride, not for you to eat,' but the lion was already loping ahead, nose to ground.

'Wait for me!' called the knight, and he ran after Arthur with long high-stepping strides like an ostrich, tripping now and then over his scabbard, and soon becoming so puffed that it was a relief to see the lion crouching not far ahead.

'Found him, master,' growled Arthur softly. 'He's just the other side of this bank. Creep up with me and peep over.'

Up they crept and over they peeped, and the knight's jaw dropped in amazement.

There before him stood a milk-white pony with a long creamy mane and a long creamy tail – as pretty a little horse as you could wish to see, yet unlike any other horse the world over. For, from the centre of its forehead, there sprouted a single sharp spiral horn!

'A unicorn!' gasped Sir Tumbleweed, leaping to his feet; and at the sound of his voice the creature whirled to face him with a snort.

It pawed the ground and lowered its head so that the sharp horn pointed directly at him, just like a lance.

'A little horse and a little lance' . . . Sir Tumbleweed's own words came back to him. Here was the perfect steed! Here was his chance to become the Champion of the Tournament! If only he could somehow persuade it to carry him.

The unicorn took several little bucketing steps forward and blew through its velvety nostrils, and the knight's newfound bravery quailed at the thought of that sharp horn sticking in his armourless body. He moved hastily behind the lion.

'What shall we do, Arthur?' he muttered.

'Flatter him,' said the lion out of the corner of his mouth. 'Everyone likes flattery but when it comes to unicorns, you can lay it on with a trowel. Start by telling him how beautiful he is.'

Sir Tumbleweed cleared his throat.

'Excuse me,' he said, 'but did anyone ever tell you how beautiful you are?'

The unicorn stopped pawing and snorting and raised his head, so that his horn no longer pointed at the knight's quaking stomach.

'Of course,' he said. 'I have often been told. But I cannot be told often enough. You may say it again.'

'You are very beautiful.'

'More beautiful than that lion?' said the unicorn.

Sir Tumbleweed hesitated. He feared to hurt Arthur's feelings.

'Say yes,' hissed the lion.

'Oh. Yes.'

'Say I'm just an old fleabag.'

'He's just an old fleabag', said the knight, 'compared to you. Such grace you have, such elegance, such an air of breeding.'

The unicorn bridled with pleasure, throwing back his pretty horned head.

'Keep it up, master,' growled Arthur.

'I've no doubt,' said Sir Tumbleweed, 'that you're sure-footed . . .'

'As a cat,' said the unicorn.

'And agile . . .'

'As a mountain goat.'

'And you can leap . . .'

'Like a deer.'

'And gallop . . .'

'Like the wind,' said the unicorn. 'I could run rings round any of those great galumphing cart-horses that people like you ride.'

'I bet you could,' said Sir Tumbleweed. 'And as for that superb horn, sharper than any lance, which you carry so proudly on your noble brow – why, I bet you could tip any old knight off his charger with that.'

'Easy as winking,' said the unicorn.

'But I don't suppose you could do it with me

on your back. You're hardly up to my weight.'

'You? A long thin fellow like you?' said the unicorn disdainfully. 'Of course I could carry you.'

'He could, master,' said Arthur.

'But would you?' said Sir Tumbleweed. 'Would you, rarest and most lovely of all animals, deign to carry an ordinary sort of chap like me?'

'I might,' said the unicorn. 'If you continue to treat me with the proper respect . . .'

'Oh, I certainly will,' said the knight. 'By the way I'm called Tumbleweed, and this is Arthur. May we be privileged to know your name?'

'I,' said the unicorn, 'am Spearhead. And don't expect me to call you "master" like that old fleabag. On the contrary, I shall expect you to obey *my* orders. For a start, go and pull me a nice bunch of that sweet long grass on the far side of the glade. Go on!'

'Oh certainly, Spearhead, certainly!' said Sir Tumbleweed, and away he strode to do the unicorn's bidding.

The lion waited until the knight was out of earshot, and then he said, 'Nice work, Spearhead.'

'I didn't overdo it, did I?' asked the unicorn anxiously.

'No,' said Arthur. 'It was just right. She'll be proud of you. Between us we'll make a Champion of him yet.'

CHAPTER 5

'Whoa, Spearhead!' cried Sir Tumbleweed.

'If you please, noblest of beasts,' he added hastily, and when the unicorn stopped he dismounted in the easiest possible manner. That is to say, he stretched his long legs, put his feet on the ground and allowed his little milk-white steed to walk out from under him.

'What's up, master?' said Arthur.

'That's up,' said the knight, pointing to a large notice nailed on a wayside tree. 'That's what I've been looking for all this time.'

For weeks now the three of them had roamed the forest glades where there was sweet grass for the unicorn, nuts and fruit and berries and wild

honey for Sir Tumbleweed and many fat deer, a
number of which fell before the mighty paws
and jaws of Arthur the lion. Arthur liked his
meat raw, but the knight preferred his venison
barbecued and flavoured with mushrooms and
herbs.

All the time Sir Tumbleweed had three things
in mind.

First, to keep out of sight of other people; he
wanted no one to know about his friends.

Second, to practise unicorn-riding; this of
course was bareback stuff – knees bent to keep
his feet from scuffing the ground, thin shanks
gripping tight, hands grasping the long creamy

mane; but already he had become quite an expert unicorn-man: expert, that is, at sticking on, which was all that he had to do.

And third, to get news, somehow, of a Tournament; the witch could have told him where to go, no doubt, but he had seen no sign of her since that first meeting.

Now here was that news!

The lion and the unicorn stood listening as he read out the notice:

OYEZ!
Grande Tournamente!
One week hence.

Take notice that there is to be a Grande Tournamente of Jousting in the Greate Meadowe by the river, near to Saint Ethelred's bridge.

Knights only need applie.
He that unhorses every opponent shall be styled the Champion of England!

Knock-off Competition.
Three jousts per knight per day.

Entrance Fee –
Ladyes and Gentilmenne: one ducat.
Squires, Freemen, Varlets, Serfs, and
other common folk: one groat.
Childer: halfe pryce.

Oxen roasted whole.
Ale and mead in ye Refreshment Tent.
Manye sideshows.

Beware Pyckpockets.

'One week hence?' said Arthur. 'Hence from whence?'

'And how far is this Saint Ethelred's bridge?' asked Spearhead.

'A goodly few leagues, I'll warrant,' said Sir Tumbleweed. 'We must hurry. Can you keep up, Arthur?'

'Not with that streak of lightning you're riding, master,' said the lion, 'but I'll follow by scent.'

'Right, Spearhead,' said Sir Tumbleweed. 'Let's go!'

He threw a long leg over the unicorn's back and grabbed hold of the creamy mane.

Spearhead made no move.

'Gee-up!' shouted the knight.

Spearhead stamped his elegant little foot, and shook his elegant little head with that slim sharp horn.

'Oh sorry!' said Sir Tumbleweed. 'I wasn't thinking!'

'If you please,' he said, 'beautiful Spearhead. Shrewdest, strongest, swiftest of beasts – gee-up!' And away they went.

High above, a great soaring bird looked down and saw with his eagle eye a rider on a white steed galloping towards the edge of the forest.

Behind them, he saw a lion trotting along on their trail.

Ahead of them, the trees ended on the rim of a valley, and in the bed of the valley was a river.

Further down the valley there was a bend in the river and within the bend, close to an old stone bridge, lay a large flat meadow, covered with many brightly coloured tents and booths and thronged with people.

Not far from the meadow was a thick wood, and into this the rider disappeared. No longer able to see him, the eagle lost interest and flew away.

'What luck, master?' panted Arthur when he arrived and looked down at the busy scene below. 'Are we in time?'

At that moment they heard the sound of a trumpet, and saw a herald ride out into the middle of the field.

'In the nick of time, I think,' said Sir Tumbleweed. 'Listen.'

'Hear ye, hear ye, good people all!' called the herald. 'Now begins the first bout of the day, between – on my right in the blue corner –' (and he pointed to a small blue tent at one edge of the field) 'Sir Thomas the Terrible!' Out from the little tent rode a knight in full armour mounted on a mighty charger, and everyone cheered like mad as he raised his lance in salute. 'And on my left in the red corner –' cried the herald, pointing the opposite way, 'Sir Frederick the Frightful!' And from a small red tent

34

appeared a second knight, whose salute was greeted once again with a roar of applause. 'The contest to be decided by a fall,' shouted the herald, 'or, failing that, by hits on helmet or shield. Blue corner – Sir Thomas! Red corner – Sir Frederick! Ready, steady, go!'

The watchers in the wood saw the two knights begin to move towards one another, at first at no more than a clumsy trot, so heavy were both horse and rider. But gradually they picked up speed, each rider holding the butt of his lance under his right forearm and aiming the shaft of it across his horse's back to strike his opponent as they passed, left side to left side.

Above the yells of the crowd and the thunder of hooves, Sir Tumbleweed and his friends could hear the almighty crash as the contestants met in the middle of the field, and one dumped the other on the seat of his steel pants.

Joust after joust the watchers saw, as knight after knight trundled across the tilting-field – to fell or be felled, to hit or to miss, to win or to lose. Big beefy chaps they were, one and all, with names like Sir Martin the Merciless, Sir Colin the Cruel, and Sir Herbert the Horrible – names to strike terror into the stoutest heart.

Sir Tumbleweed's began to feel less stout by the minute.

Whose stupid idea was this anyway, he thought; can't have been mine, must have been the witch's. But I don't expect I'll ever see her again. If I just keep quiet a bit longer, the Tournament will be over and it'll be too late for me to take part.

He glanced sideways at his companions. The lion lay gazing down at the scene, head on paws. The unicorn stood watching intently, like a little white statue. Both seemed to have forgotten about him.

At that moment the trumpet rang out again,

and the herald rode in, flanked by two very large knights on horses like elephants, one brown, one piebald.

'My Lords, Ladyes, and Gentilmenne!' shouted the herald. 'This is the Final Joust for the Heavyweight Championship of all England, between the only two contestants as yet undefeated in today's Tournament! Introducing – on my left – representing Northumbria – and weighing in at One Tun and Seven Hundreds of Weight – the moody, the masterful, the magnificent – SIR DENYS THE DEADLY!!'

There was a huge roar of applause.

'And on my right – representing Wessex – and weighing in at One Tun and Eight and One Half Hundreds of Weight – the fearsome, the furious, the fantabulous – SIR BASIL THE BEASTLY!!'

The herald waited till the cheering had once again died away.

'He that first unhorses his opponent,' he finally cried, 'shall be declared the Champion! To your corners, gentilmenne! Come out fighting, and may the best knight win!'

The crowd fell silent as the two finalists took up their positions.

They turned to face one another, lances and shields at the ready, and each pulled down the visor of his helmet with an ominous clang.

Then, at the tootle of the trumpet, Sir Denys and Sir Basil set spurs to their chargers.

'I fancy the piebald!' said Spearhead.

'I fancy the brown!' said Arthur.

I don't fancy either, thought Sir Tumbleweed. Doesn't make much odds whether it's One Tun and Seven Hundreds of Weight or One Tun and Eight and One Half if it hits you smack on the button, and he shut his eyes.

When he opened them again, it was to see Sir Denys flat on his back, and Sir Basil galumphing triumphantly around the meadow on a lap of honour. At last, to the cheers of the crowd, Sir Basil drew to a halt in the centre of the tilting-field, removed his helmet, disclosing a big beefy face on top of his big beefy body on top of his huge hairy horse, and bawled, 'I am the Champion!'

Sir Tumbleweed gave a sigh of relief.

'Oh goody,' he said, 'it's over. We can go now, can't we?'

Arthur did not move, but Spearhead came immediately to stand ready beside the knight.

'Of course,' he said. 'Jump on.'

But as soon as Sir Tumbleweed was mounted, the unicorn carried him out of the wood, straight down to the Greate Meadowe by the river, near to Saint Ethelred's bridge, and through the astonished crowd and on to the tilting-field.

'Stop!' cried Sir Tumbleweed, tugging madly at the creamy mane of his steed, 'Please, Spearhead, stop!'

But to his horror, the unicorn broke from a walk to a trot and from a trot to a canter, and then they were at full speed, galloping straight towards the Champion.

CHAPTER 6

Just when it seemed that they must crash straight into the Champion, Spearhead slid to a dramatic halt. He reared up on his hindlegs (with Sir Tumbleweed clinging desperately around his neck), flourished his little forefeet in the very face of Sir Basil's great piebald charger, and gave a shrill neigh of defiance.

The sound died away, and there was a moment of absolute silence around the tilting-field.

Then Sir Basil the Beastly found his voice. A big beefy voice it was, and an angry one too, for the new Champion was not best pleased thus to be interrupted at his time of greatest glory.

'Away with you, fellow!' he shouted. 'Begone!'

Sir Tumbleweed did not reply, for two simple reasons. One, he could think of nothing to say, and two, he very much wanted to be gone. Jousting suddenly looked much less fun.

He hauled urgently at the unicorn's mane, but Spearhead took no notice of him, pawing at the ground and tossing his head with its slim sharp horn.

'Are you deaf?' bawled Sir Basil, and the crowd began to laugh.

To his great surprise, Sir Tumbleweed felt himself becoming angry.

'No,' he said, 'I'm not. So there's no need to shout.'

At this the crowd's laughter turned to a babble of excitement. Who was this man rash enough to answer back to the Champion? Such a long skinny creature, with a tousled head of red hair and a droopy red moustache and no armour and only a pony to ride – why, Sir Basil would kill him for his impudence!

'I'll kill you for your impudence!' bellowed Sir Basil. 'You common clown!'

And silence fell again in the crowd, a crowd that had swelled as stallholders left their booths and sideshows, squires left their knights, grooms their chargers, and everyone came running from outlying parts of the Greate Meadowe to watch this strange confrontation, while the pyckpockets moved easily among them.

Among them, too, unnoticed in the crush, was a figure dressed all in black, with a tall black hat upon its head and a long black cloak, against whose hem a black cat rubbed itself. Above the black scarf that hid the face, a pair of grey eyes twinkled at Sir Tumbleweed's next words.

'You mistake me,' he said, in a quiet voice that all could none the less hear. 'I am not a common clown. I am a knight.'

The Champion burst into a big beefy roar of laughter.

'A knight!' he said. 'You! A long cold stream of pump water like you!' The crowd sniggered. 'What's your name then?'

'Tumbleweed,' said Sir Tumbleweed, and the crowd rocked with mirth.

'Tumbleweed!' they cried to each other. 'He be a weed and no mistake, and Sir Basil will soon tumble 'ee!'

Faced with the insults of the Champion and

the mockery of the onlookers, Sir Tumbleweed
threw caution to the winds. He waited till the
laughter had died down, and then he called out,
loudly and clearly, 'And I challenge you!'

He waited a few seconds while the crowd
caught its breath, and then he added, 'Fatface!'

Sir Basil the Beastly fairly gobbled with rage.

'You . . . you challenge me?' he spluttered.
'You are a fool!'

'And you', said Sir Tumbleweed, 'are a bigger
one, so yah-boo and sucks to you!' He put his
thumbs in his ears and waggled his fingers and

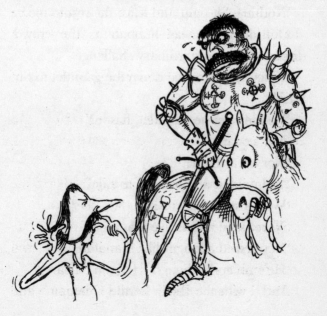

stuck his tongue out, while a great roar went up from the crowd, which was now so excited that they did not hear an echoing roar roll down from the thick wood above the tilting-field.

Once inside the little tent in the red corner, Sir Tumbleweed leaned forward and spoke into the ear of his steed.

'I didn't overdo it, did I?' he asked anxiously.

'No,' said Spearhead. 'You've got him so mad he can't see straight. He'll be a pushover.'

'What d'you want me to do?'

'Nothing. Sit tight and leave the rest to me.'

Outside there was hubbub as the crowd discussed the extraordinary challenge.

'Fancy 'im throwing down the gauntlet to Sir Basil!'

'He ain't got no gauntlet, has 'e?'

'Nor no lance!'

'Nor no armour!'

'And nobbut a little pony to ride!'

'With a spike on its head, didst see?'

'Never seed a hoss like that afore!'

'Never seed a knight like that afore!'

'He's got spirit though. He bain't afeared!'

And when the herald began his

announcement and the challenger rode out of the tent to stand ready, there were many voices cheering on the underdog as Englishmen do.

'Good luck, sir!' they cried, and 'Never worry – we'll give thee decent burial!'

When at last the trumpet blew, the unicorn set off at full gallop. He covered the ground so speedily that Sir Basil and his charger had hardly begun to trundle when Spearhead was upon them, Sir Tumbleweed bent low on his neck so that the point of the Champion's lance passed harmlessly over him.

Nimble as a cat, the unicorn turned in his tracks and set off in pursuit of the ponderous pair.

Down came his head as they closed, and into the big piebald bottom went the sharp little horn, and up went the charger's heels in a great startled buck-jump, and over his head sailed Sir Basil the Beastly, to land with a noise like seventy steel saucepans falling on a flagstoned floor.

Spearhead slid to a halt beside the fallen Champion, and Sir Tumbleweed stepped off, drawing his sword. He bent down and raised the visor of Sir Basil's helmet.

'Say you're sorry,' he said.

'What for?' growled Sir Basil dazedly.

'For calling me a long cold stream of pump water.'

'Shan't,' said Sir Basil, struggling furiously but vainly to get up.

'All right,' said Sir Tumbleweed. 'Just you watch this then.'

He pulled Sir Basil's sword from its scabbard, and with one blow of his own weapon, he cut it in half.

Then he quartered his shield.

Then he chopped his lance into eight neat pieces.

'Now then,' he said pleasantly. 'A nice big carcass like you should make sixteen joints easily. What shall we begin with? An arm? A leg? Or would you prefer me to start with your head?'

'Oh no, no, no!' gasped Sir Basil. 'I'm sorry! I'm sorry!'

'And I'm not a fool?'

'No!'

'Nor a common clown?'

'No! No!'

'What am I then?' said Sir Tumbleweed.

Sir Basil the Beastly gulped.

'You are a knight,' he muttered.

'And my name?'

'Sir Tumbleweed.'

'And my title?'

'The Champion of all England,' said Sir Basil in a strangled voice.

Sir Tumbleweed motioned to the crowd to be silent and then he said, 'Say it again nice and loud, so that everyone can hear.'

Sir Basil drew a deep unhappy breath.

'You are Sir Tumbleweed,' he shouted

desperately, 'the Champion of all England!'

Sir Tumbleweed sheathed his sword.

'That's better,' he said, and he bent down once more to the helmet of the fallen knight.

'And now,' he said, 'you can shut your face.' And he closed the visor with a snap.

CHAPTER 7

Round the Great Meadowe rode the new Champion, feeling very pleased with himself and waving happily to the wildly cheering crowd.

'I say, this is fun, isn't it!' he cried to Spearhead. 'Everybody seems so pleased for me.'

'Not everybody,' said the unicorn. 'Look over there.'

Sir Tumbleweed stared across the tilting-field and saw a body of horsemen in full armour approaching at a slow deliberate walk. Among them he recognized, by the emblems on their shields and on top of their helmets, Sir Denys the Deadly, Sir Herbert the Horrible, Sir Colin the Cruel, Sir Martin the Merciless, Sir Frederick the Frightful and Sir Thomas the Terrible – to name but a few.

'Why, it's all the other contestants in the Tournament,' he said.

'Yes,' said Spearhead.

'Coming to congratulate me.'

'No,' said Spearhead.

Sir Tumbleweed looked more carefully at the riders. None, he saw, now held a lance, but each, he noticed, carried either a sharp sword, or a mighty mace, or a fearsome flail, or a

bloodthirsty-looking battleaxe.

'Oh,' said Sir Tumbleweed. 'You mean . . .'

'I mean,' said the unicorn, 'that the gentlemen bearing down upon us may not be very happy about the outcome of the Tournament or the manner of our victory. They may perhaps consider that we did not stick strictly to the Rules of Jousting. They may wish to complain.'

'There are thirty or forty of them,' said Sir Tumbleweed thoughtfully.

'Yes.'

'Perhaps we had better . . .'

'Better what?'

'Withdraw?' said Sir Tumbleweed hopefully.

Spearhead gave a snort.

'Sir Tumbleweed!' he said scornfully. 'The Champion of all England. The bravest of the brave. Retreating in the face of the foe? How could you hold your head up for the rest of your life if we ran away?'

Sir Tumbleweed looked anxiously at the oncoming knights, now but a stone's throw distant.

'If we don't,' he said, 'the rest of my life's about one minute long, after which I shan't have a head to hold up,' and he drew his sword.

At the very instant that he did so, the troop of knights reined to a halt as one man. Many pushed back their visors the better to see and their faces, as they stared in his direction, appeared not angry but worried.

At the same time the crowd around the Great Meadowe began to melt away, streaming across Saint Ethelred's bridge and disappearing into the distance as fast as their legs would carry them. Only a solitary black-garbed figure still remained, concealed within one of the booths, to see the body of knights wheel their chargers and ride hastily away after the departed spectators.

Sir Tumbleweed stared in amazement at the deserted tilting-field.

'Well I'm blowed!' he said to Spearhead. 'What d'you make of that? Who'd have thought that the whole blooming lot would have shoved off in a panic just because I drew my sword! But that's what it must have been, eh? It can't have been anything else.'

'That's what it must have been, master,' rumbled a deep voice just behind him. 'It can't have been anything else.'

Sir Tumbleweed's fame spread about the country like wildfire and, as the story passed from one to another, so it grew.

This red-haired giant of a knight, tall as a tree, had flown – yes flown – into the Greate Meadowe on a winged white beast as swift as an arrow. He had tipped the mighty Sir Basil the Beastly off his charger with one prod of his finger, then sliced him into small pieces. Finally, when a hundred, nay two hundred knights had

dared to confront him, he had called to his aid a gigantic man-eating lion!

It was not surprising, therefore, that as Sir Tumbleweed and his two companions moved about the countryside, everyone gave them a wide berth.

The mere sight of the fearsome warrior approaching sent peasants scuttling for their huts and hovels, and any gentleman who espied the terrible trio seemed suddenly to remember some pressing business in the opposite direction.

All this was bad for Sir Tumbleweed.

His victory in the Tournament and the routing of the other knights (for both of which he now gave himself the credit rather than the unicorn and the lion), combined with the awe in which he was so plainly held, went to his head. It swelled, and his behaviour became hard to bear.

He would shout insults at any knight they chanced to meet, calling him rude names like 'Sir Potbelly' or 'Sir Bigbum', and when the rider made off, rather than face the fabled might of the Champion, Sir Tumbleweed would jeer at him. 'Cowardy cowardy custard, wouldn't eat the mustard!' he would shout, with a self-satisfied grin on his once gloomy face. Even his moustache began to look different, for he had taken to brushing the ends of it upwards in a fierce fashion.

It was plain to Arthur and Spearhead that the knight had grown much too big for his boots, and needed taking down a peg if he were not to become quite unbearable. They discussed the matter while Sir Tumbleweed slept.

'What he needs,' said Spearhead, 'is a short sharp shock.'

'Like fighting for his life . . .' said Arthur.

'Without us to help him . . .' said Spearhead.

'Against something really terrifying . . .' said Arthur.

'A dragon for example . . .'

'Yes, a simply huge fire-breathing one . . .'

'With great leathery wings . . .'

'And a long lashing tail . . .'

'And terrible claws . . .'

'And horrible teeth!'

'Right,' said Spearhead. 'That's settled.'

'That'll teach him to be so cocky,' said Arthur. Both animals thought with pleasure about this plan, in a silence broken only by Sir Tumbleweed's snores and a little scratching noise somewhere near by, the sort of noise a cat makes sharpening its claws on a tree.

'That only leaves us one thing to do then,' said Spearhead.

'Yes,' said Arthur. 'We need to find a nice fierce dragon.'

'That might be arranged,' said a low pleasant voice in the darkness of the windy night.

CHAPTER 8

So it came as no surprise to Arthur and Spearhead when, next morning, they just happened to run across a dragon.

Sir Tumbleweed had woken feeling very full of himself. He'd had a delicious dream about a delicious damsel in distress (whom he had of course rescued with the utmost ease), and he was generally so pleased with life that, as they travelled on, he burst into song.

For both the lion and the unicorn, this was painful, partly because the knight's voice was loud and rather tuneless, but mostly because he sang, as usual, the same song of his own invention, over and over again.

Who is the most courageous knight (he sang)
Of all that noble band?
Whose is the sword most sharp and bright
Grasped in whose sturdy hand?
Whose intellect, whose wit, whose might,
Whose skill can none withstand?
Who is it no one dares to fight
Throughout old England's la-a-and?

(and then the chorus, which was . . .)

Sir Tumbleweed! Sir Tumbleweed!
High let his banner wave!
Sir Tumbleweed! Sir Tumbleweed!
The bravest of the brave!

He was just beginning it for the fourth time as they approached a narrow rocky ravine, when the unicorn stopped in his tracks, nostrils flaring.

Beside him the lion lifted his great head, the better to test the wind.

Both could plainly recognize the scent that was wafted on it.

A very strong scent it was, part beast, part bird, part fish; a kind of mixture of the smells

58

you might find in a pigsty, in a chicken-house
and on a fishmonger's slab on a hot day, topped
with a faint tang of smoke.

'What's the matter?' asked Sir Tumbleweed,
as the two animals stood motionless but for the
nervous stamp of Spearhead's forefoot.

'There's danger ahead, master,' growled
Arthur softly.

'Danger?' said 'the most courageous knight
of all that noble band'. 'Don't talk such piffle,
Arthur. What could be a danger to me?' And he
brushed up the ends of his moustache with one
hand and drew his sword with the other, jutting

out his long jaw and throwing back his head proudly as he stared ahead.

On his face was the confident smile of a man 'whose skill can none withstand'.

'Forward!' he cried, but Spearhead took no notice.

'Oh all right, if you must have it,' said Sir Tumbleweed, 'forward, please.' But still the unicorn did not move.

'Arthur!' said the knight sharply. 'Go and see what it is. Go on, boy, quick!' But the lion only lashed his tail and looked sulky.

Sir Tumbleweed dismounted.

'What a lily-livered pair you are!' he said scornfully. 'I can see I'll have to go and deal with this "danger" by myself. It's probably a great big ferocious rabbit,' and he strode forward towards the rim of the ravine.

Halfway there, he looked back expecting to see his companions watching him admiringly, but they had vanished. Cowards, thought Sir Tumbleweed, and began to sing the chorus of his song.

Just then the smell hit him. It was so strong, and somehow so threatening a smell that something told 'the most courageous knight' discretion might be the better part of valour. He stopped singing and, sheathing his sword, began to crawl forward on hands and knees.

Reaching the edge of the ravine, Sir Tumbleweed peered cautiously over. Immediately below him lay a very large dragon.

As it happened, Sir Tumbleweed had never before in his life set eyes upon a dragon, though recently he had often dreamed of meeting one (a smallish, cowardly sort of one that would give him no trouble). Never in his wildest nightmares had he imagined such a dragon as this was.

To begin with, it was so long, about as long as

three lions laid end to end. And everything about it was much too big for comfort – wings, tail, claws, teeth. Its lizardly skin was red – not the jolly carroty red of the knight's hair and moustache – but a dreadful red, the colour of hot new-spilled blood. At each breath, two puffs of smoke rose from nostrils that looked, from above, like the craters of twin volcanoes.

The only good thing, to Sir Tumbleweed's mind, was that the volcanoes seemed to be dormant, for the monster's eyes were shut and it was deep in slumber. Let sleeping dragons lie, thought the knight. I'll tell the others it was a dead one, it pongs bad enough to be, and he begun to squirm backwards.

Clumsy as ever, he managed to dislodge a stone which rolled over the rim of the ravine and fell, striking the dragon neatly on top of the head.

The volcanic eruption that resulted was horrific!

In one lightning movement the creature sprang to its four feet, spreading its wings and lashing its tail, and opened wide both its eyes and its mouth, from which shot a great orange jet of flame.

To the reek of dragon was added now the smell of singed hair as the flame whooshed above Sir Tumbleweed's head.

There was a moment's silence, broken only by the crackling of burning bushes, and then the dragon spoke.

'You up there!' it said. 'Come down by here, look you! Quickly now, whoever you are, or it's fried you'll be, see?'

Curiously the dragon had a lilting sing-song voice, high-pitched and with an unfamiliar accent, but in his state of shock the knight did not notice this: too many thoughts were rushing through his head, all of them uncomfortable.

What a fool I am, he thought miserably, what a boastful big-headed fool; and now it's out of the frying-pan and into the fire, and serve me jolly well right, and I shan't half miss old Arthur and young Spearhead, and that witch too in a funny sort of way, and now I shall never rescue a damsel and live happily ever after because I'm going to die – unhappily – right now.

Strangely, the last of these thoughts made Sir Tumbleweed feel suddenly calm, and he got to his feet, determined that if he must fry, at least he would fry like a man! He stared down at the great red dragon just below and called out, in the boldest voice he could muster, 'Listen to me and I'll give you a piece of advice.'

The dragon stared up at him, fumes curling from its nostrils.

'Advice, is it?' it said. 'There's cheeky! And what advice is that, boyo?'

'Give up smoking,' said Sir Tumbleweed. 'It's bad for your health.'

CHAPTER 9

'Bad for my health indeed!' cried the dragon. 'I'll tell you somethin', look you – my smokin' is goin' to be very bad for your health, whatever! Next time, I'll do more than singe your whiskers!'

Sir Tumbleweed put up a hand and felt his moustache. It was indeed a good deal shorter, and this made him angry. That moustache had taken a long time to grow to such a length, and in addition he had just spent a lot of effort in training it to curl up rather than down.

He forgot all about the very real probability of being burned to death, and began to climb

down the side of the ravine as fast as he could
in order to confront the dragon.

(Hidden among bushes on the opposite edge,
the lion and the unicorn watched and listened.)

Sir Tumbleweed stumped up to the dragon in
a proper tizzy, and stood before it, arms akimbo.

'Look here, whatsyername . . .' he said.

'Jones,' said the dragon.

'Look here, Jones . . .'

'*Mister* Jones,' said the dragon.

'Oh, very well, if you must – look here,
Mister Jones, you've burned the ends of my
moustache off! What did you want to do that
for?'

'Throwin' stones at me you were,' said Mister Jones.

'I wasn't,' said Sir Tumbleweed. 'I didn't mean to. I looked over and saw you and I thought I'd better . . .'

'Better what?'

'. . . withdraw.'

'Run away, you mean.'

'Well, crawl away.'

'A coward is it you are then?' said the dragon. (Arthur and Spearhead looked at one another.)

'Yes,' said Sir Tumbleweed slowly. 'I am a coward. Still. Sometimes.'

('Give him credit,' said Spearhead softly, 'he's got the courage to admit it.')

('And to stand face to face with one of the biggest dragons that ever came out of Wales,' murmured Arthur.)

'I thought I heard you singin' just now,' said the dragon. 'Somethin' about "the bravest of the brave"?'

'How could you have?' said the knight. 'You were asleep.'

'Pretendin',' said Mister Jones. 'I was listenin', really. Fond of music I am, see. A light tenor myself. Though I've heard better voices than yours, boyo, I'm bound to say. Tone deaf you are, see, and no mistake. Tumbleweed is it they call you?'

'Sir Tumbleweed,' said the knight.

'Oh sorry,' said Mister Jones. 'You don't look like a knight. They usually come tinned. Easier for cookin', see. Now you, I'll have to be careful not to frizzle you up. Not much fat on you at all. Tell the truth, you're not worth lightin' the fire for, there's not enough meat in the sausage.'

'You mean you're not going to kill me?' said Sir Tumbleweed.

'No,' said Mister Jones. 'I'm sparin' your life, see. On one condition.'

'What's that?'

'Give up singin'. It's bad for my ears.'

Sir Tumbleweed stopped being angry and started to giggle. He suddenly found this quaintly-spoken Welsh dragon extremely comical, and the giggle turned into a chortle and the chortle into peals of laughter.

'What's funny, boyo?' said Mister Jones, his scaly brow furrowed in puzzlement.

'You-hoo-hoo are!' hooted Sir Tumbleweed. 'You sound f-funny and you look f-funny, and who-hoo-hoo ever heard of a dragon called Mister Jo-ho-hones!!' And he laughed so much that he had to lie down.

As Arthur and Spearhead made their descent into the ravine, they met the dragon coming up. Hastily, they introduced themselves.

'Pleased to meet you,' said Mister Jones. 'She told me you were with him, see. Havin' some kind of fit he is.'

Below them Sir Tumbleweed rolled about on the ground holding his ribs, while the tears ran down his face.

'I didn't overdo it, did I?' asked the dragon anxiously.

'No,' said Spearhead. 'It's just what we wanted. You forced him to admit he's not as brave as he makes out.'

'And we heard that,' said Arthur.

'And you've stopped him singing.'

'So we shan't have to hear that again.'

The red dragon shook his head in bewilderment.

'There's curious,' he said. 'Laughin' at my name he was, see. Soft in the head is he now?'

'Soft in the heart,' said the lion. 'He's looking for a damsel in distress, so that he can rescue her and marry her.'

'You don't happen to know of a local one, shut up in a castle somewhere, do you?' asked the unicorn. 'Preferably guarded by a smallish dragon that our man could handle?'

'A non-smoker, if possible,' said the lion.

'The country's so thickly forested,' the unicorn said, 'that castles with damsels in them are hard to find.'

Mister Jones considered.

'What you need, I'm thinkin',' he said, 'is an aerial survey, see? And for that, I'm your dragon. Watch this now.'

The lion and the unicorn watched as, with

much flapping, the red dragon took off. Once airborne, he spread his leathery wings wide and called down to them: 'Know what they call me back home?'

'No,' they shouted. 'What?'

'Jones the Jet,' he cried, and opening his mouth to emit a great gush of flame, shot off at high speed, backwards.

CHAPTER 10

For many days and nights Mister Jones jetted about the skies above the English countryside, looking for damsels.

One good burn was enough to propel him a long way, and while he glided thus, he sang. Mostly he sang in Welsh, and many a terrified peasant herding his beasts cowered in horror as a great spread-winged shape, carolling blithely in a strange tongue, swept over him tail-first at treetop height.

Then the weird words would give place to a dreadful rushing roar as the dragon blasted off once more to gain altitude, while the frantic flocks and herds stampeded in all directions.

Every now and again, Mister Jones would be reminded by the sight of the fleeing animals that his fires needed stoking, and would land for a snack. A bullock, say, or half a dozen sheep.

Helpless peasants were one thing, well-armed noblemen in well-defended fortresses another, and each time that the dragon came across a likely-looking castle, it was to find the occupants fully prepared. The sheep and cattle would have been driven inside the castle walls, the drawbridge pulled up and the portcullis let down, and every man would stand to his arms. If Mister Jones swooped down too close, he would be met by a shower of arrows – not that that worried him much for he was too thick-skinned.

But still he did not find what he was looking for, a damsel in distress for Sir Tumbleweed to rescue.

A damsel in distress, he knew, was always shut up in the highest room of the tallest tower, leaning out of the window waving a handkerchief.

Once, he did find someone doing this, but when he glided closer he saw that she was an old stout serving-wench shaking out a duster.

'Be off with you, you nasty old crow!' she shouted, proving herself not to be a distressed damsel – and that she was short-sighted and colour-blind to boot.

While Mister Jones was conducting his aerial survey, Sir Tumbleweed and his companions continued their search on foot. Castles apart, there was always the chance that they might happen upon an unhappy maiden tied to a tree, or imprisoned in a cave, or marooned on an island in a river.

But though they had no luck, they were quite content. There was no hurry, the weather was fine, and as time passed the relationship between the three of them became increasingly close.

To some extent this was the result of a conversation they had at the end of a pleasantly tiring day's travel.

The man was sitting and the two beasts lying on the soft springy turf beneath a big beech tree, in whose canopy birds sang happy-sounding songs. The evening was sunny, and the knight felt specially happy as he sat between his fellow-travellers.

One carries me and one guards me in my quest, he thought, and neither ever complains.

He patted the unicorn's milk-white flank.

'Not too tired, Spearhead, I hope?' he said. 'But then you wouldn't be, you've such strength and such stamina.'

The unicorn turned his head, its elegant spiral horn glinting in the light of the westering sun.

'I think it's about time,' he said, 'that you stopped all this business of buttering me up with compliments. We know each other well enough now, don't you think?'

'We do,' said Sir Tumbleweed. 'And I know myself much better too. I'm afraid I became dreadfully big-headed when all the time it was you who won the Tournament for me; and you, Arthur,' and he stroked the lion's curly mane, 'who saw off the knights. I suppose it was meeting that comical Welsh beast and realizing that after all I'm still a nervous knight that brought me to my senses. Nice chap though, Mister Jones. Lucky that I should have bumped into such a decent dragon.'

'Lucky indeed, master,' said Arthur.

'That's another thing,' said Sir Tumbleweed.

'I think it's also about time you packed in calling me "master". I'm not your master. We're just three chums.'

'What shall I call you then?' asked the lion.

'What did your friends call you?' asked the unicorn.

'Friends?'

'Amongst the other knights?'

'I didn't really have any friends, I'm afraid. The others either laughed at me for being clumsy or sneered at me for being nervous.'

'Well, what about your parents?' said Spearhead. 'What did your mother call you when you were small?'

Sir Tumbleweed looked a trifle embarrassed.

'Mummy called me Tummy,' he said.

'That's a nice name,' they both replied, straightfaced.

'D'you really think so?' said Sir Tumbleweed. 'In that case, do please feel free to use it!'

So they did.

The very next morning, as it happened, they were woken by the sound of singing. It was not the birds at their dawn chorus, but a fine ringing tenor voice high in the sky above.

Has anyone seen Sir Tumbleweed?
A knight that is tall and thin.
He's different, see, from other knights,
A tunic he wears, and a pair of tights,
Instead of a suit of tin.

They ran out from beneath the beech tree and gazed up, to see Mister Jones gliding along some way away, and as they watched, he sang another verse:

If anyone sees Sir Tumbleweed
Remember now, don't forget
To tell him, see, there's no time to lose
And hurry he must, for there's lovely news
Arrivin' by Jones the Jet.

By the end of this second verse the dragon was near enough to hear the row they were making in order to attract his attention. Sir Tumbleweed shouted, Spearhead neighed, Arthur roared and, catching sight of them, Mister Jones banked. After a short burn to clear the treetops, he made a perfect five-point (including his tail) landing beside them.

'There's glad I am to see you!' he cried. 'Singin' that song over and over again I've been. Lucky it is I have a fireproof throat, or sore it would be by now.'

Sir Tumbleweed felt very pleased to see the red dragon again, despite his fearful smell.

'This news, this lovely news!' he cried. 'You've found me a damsel?'

'Absolutely, boyo.'

'In distress?'

'No doubt about it. Leanin' from a turret window she was, look you, wavin' her little hanky and callin' out.'

'What was she calling?'

'"Help!" and "Save me!" You can't say much plainer than that, can you now?'

Sir Tumbleweed cleared his throat.

'What have I got to save her from?' he asked.

'That I couldn't tell you,' said Mister Jones. 'Moonlight it was, see; big blotches of shadow everywhere. Probably one of my English cousins. Useful dragons in their way, though not a patch on us Welsh.'

'Don't worry, Tummy,' said Spearhead. 'You'll be a match for it, whatever it is.'

'Yes,' growled Arthur. 'You'll soon put paid to it with that sword of yours, Tummy. Then you can marry the beautiful maiden.'

'She was beautiful, was she?' said Sir Tumbleweed eagerly.

'Bless you,' said Mister Jones, 'I couldn't have told you that if it had been broad daylight. Dragons now, it's easy to see who's good-lookin' and who's ugly. Look at me now.'

They looked at him, and wondered.

'But humans, why they're all the same to me, barrin' some are hairier round the face. How's your whiskers by the way, boyo? Growin' again?'

Sir Tumbleweed twisted his moustache proudly. The singeing it had received from the dragon had done it a power of good, and he had trained it into a really fierce shape.

'It's grown again very nicely, thank you, Mister Jones,' he said.

The dragon lowered his head to peer more closely at the knight's face. Fortunately his breath, unlike the rest of him, did not smell bad, but when he spoke the knight felt as though an oven door had suddenly opened.

'Look see, boyo,' he said, 'you can drop the "Mister" if you want. Just between friends like. As I said, folk generally call me Jones the Jet, but to my real pals I'm Taffy, see?'

As well as the heat from the dragon's breath, Sir Tumbleweed felt a glow of inner warmth.

'Thanks, Taffy,' he said.

'Don't mention it, Tummy,' said the dragon, and the four friends all laughed happily together.

CHAPTER 11

The knight, the unicorn and the lion were following the trail that the dragon had blazed.

'Is it far, this castle?' Sir Tumbleweed had asked the previous evening.

'An hour's flyin' time, no more. By jet, that is,' said Taffy Jones.

'So a good few days' march for us?'

'No doubt about that, Tummy. But at least I can show you the direct route. Straight line, see. Shortest distance between two points, look you.'

'You mean that you're going to walk straight from here to there?'

'Bless you, no,' said the dragon. 'Walkin's a terrible trial to me, I'm too heavy, see. It's all this

meat-eatin'; I must go on a diet one of these days. No, no, I'll fly there, and as I go, I'll blaze a trail for you to follow.'

'How do you mean?' asked Sir Tumbleweed.

'Well, I'll fly really low, see – hedge-hoppin', we call it – and every so often, every couple of hundred yards or much further if it's open country, I'll switch on my ignition. Dual-purpose that will be, carryin' me forward at a good rate of knots, and at the same time burnin' a spot on the ground beneath me to keep you on course. That's what I mean by blazin' a trail. If you see a patch of blackened grass or a little tree a bit toasted, you'll know you're goin' straight. You'll have to keep your eyes skinned, mind – I'll only give a little squirt each time, just to make a small mark: we don't want a forest fire.'

'Sounds brilliant,' said Sir Tumbleweed. 'Can we start tomorrow?'

'Sooner the better, boyo,' said Mister Jones. 'You don't want to get there and find she's already been rescued, do you now?'

The scheme was working well. Arthur padded ahead, his good nose telling him of charred twigs or leaves or burned grass, and Spearhead followed carrying the knight.

Up hill and down dale they went, straight as a die across the rolling countryside, all that day and for many days after, following the trail. And all the time Sir Tumbleweed's mind was full of the damsel ahead. He could picture her perfectly. She would be tall, as he had told the witch (it was fortunate that she had had grey eyes – they were his favourite) but there were other things about her that he had been too tactful to mention in front of such an ugly person.

Her hair – it would be smooth and golden and very long.

Her nose – it would be straight, perhaps even a little aquiline, a noble nose.

Her mouth would be a perfect little rosebud.

And her cheeks would be exquisitely pale, as befitted a lady careful to guard her complexion from the cold winds or the heat of the sun.

Indeed, once or twice he was so lost in thought that he forgot to duck as they passed beneath low branches and was swept off the unicorn's back, but he hardly noticed the odd bruise so rapt was he in his daydream.

'A groat for your thoughts, Tummy,' Spearhead would say, but the knight only smiled and shook his head.

For a week and more they pressed on, till at last one evening they reached their journey's end.

Sir Tumbleweed was riding in a trance as usual when suddenly Spearhead stopped as they were descending a steep slope, so that the knight had to grab the horn to save himself from sliding over the head of his steed.

Righting himself, he looked up to see the lion climbing back towards them at a swinging trot.

'I think we've arrived, Tummy,' Arthur said. 'At the lower end of this valley there's a castle. It's getting too dark to see clearly, but I could hear a voice calling.'

'A female voice, Arthur?'

'Yes.'

'Calling "Help!" and "Save me!"?'

'Yes.'

'Oh goody goody!'

They followed Arthur down the bed of the valley to a point where there was one last little patch of burned bushes, and ahead, sure enough, they could just make out the shape of a

castle's battlements. One specially tall turret stood black against the sky, and from it they could hear the cries for aid.

There was just enough light left to see a huge shape sprawled before the castle gates, its back towards them; and the wind brought a familiar smell.

'Oh look!' said Sir Tumbleweed, dismounting. 'There's good old Mister Jones waiting for us!'

Spearhead began to crop the grass, and the sight of someone else eating stirred the knight's appetite.

'Tell you what, Arthur,' he said. 'You go and catch us something nice to eat, and then our Welsh friend can barbecue it for us. I'll just pop down and invite him to supper,' and off he strode. As he neared the shadowy form, he thought it might be rather fun to creep up on Taffy Jones and make him jump. He tiptoed forward, and when he reached the dragon's tail he drew his sword. Prodding the tail with the tip of the blade, Sir Tumbleweed cried, 'Boo!'

This time, there was no volcanic eruption. Instead the dragon rose to its feet very slowly, and turned around very slowly to face him.

'Hullo, Taffy!' said the knight cheerily. 'It's me, Tummy. We've arrived. Come and have something to eat.'

The voice that replied from the darkness was a very deep bass voice, with no hint of a Welsh accent.

'Something . . . to . . . eat?' it said, very slowly. 'It appears . . . to me . . . that supper . . . is . . . already served.'

CHAPTER 12

Sir Tumbleweed's immediate and almost over-powering instinct was to run for it as fast as his long legs would carry him, but just at that instant there came another heart-rending cry for help from the turret high above.

The sound of the cry, coupled with the certainty that he would be fried the moment he turned to flee, decided him not to.

He thought fast. This dragon, from the slowness of its speech and movement, sounded pretty thick. He must play for time.

'So you eat people, do you?' he said in a light conversational tone. 'Frightfully bad for you, you know.'

For a moment there was no reply. By now a full moon had risen, and by its brilliant light Sir Tumbleweed could see that this dragon was much like Mister Jones to look at, save for its colour which was green. The dragon looked puzzled.

Then it said, 'Why . . . is eating people . . . bad . . . for me?'

'Rots your teeth,' said Sir Tumbleweed, 'and gives you awful bad breath.'

The green dragon thought about this for a while.

Then it said, 'I only . . . eat . . . the . . . best people.'

This was patently true. The evidence was plain to see, scattered around. The moonlight glinted on swords and maces and battle-axes, on lances and plumed helmets and emblazoned shields; the last relics of long-digested knights.

'The best people,' Sir Tumbleweed said, 'are the worst for your teeth. Chewing up all that armour ruins 'em.'

'Is . . . that . . . so?' said the dragon. 'All the more reason . . . then . . . to eat you. You've got . . . no . . . armour,' and it opened its mouth wide.

Afterwards, looking back on that desperate moment, Sir Tumbleweed found it hard to believe that he, the nervous knight, could ever have acted with such coolness, with such decision, with such speed.

At death's door, alone, with no hope of help from his friends, at last he found that precious gift for which he had always longed: true courage.

Moving like lightning, all his clumsiness forgotten, he snatched up a lance from the ground and thrust it into the dragon's gaping mouth, setting it upright between upper and lower jaw to prop them open. Then he grabbed a round shield and jammed it into the monster's throat. There it lodged, a steel fire-door to protect him from the furnace within – and not a moment too soon. To the sound of a terrible internal roaring and rumbling the metal began

to change colour, first to a dull, then to a brilliant red, as the dragon tried vainly to blast the knight; until at last its slow brain registered the pain in its throat, and, turning clumsily, it waddled into the moat and stuck its head under.

Fortune favours the brave, they say, and it was Sir Tumbleweed's good luck (for the drawbridge was raised) that here now was a live pontoon over which to cross the water.

Nimbly he climbed upon the dragon's back and scampered along it.

Athletically he leaped the final gap on to the apron of the drawbridge.

Acrobatically he shinned up the ivied wall of the gatehouse.

Gymnastically he balanced on the very topmost edge of the raised drawbridge itself, and looked down.

Immediately below, the dragon raised its dripping head. Somehow it had got rid of both lance and shield, and it stared at him with eyes that blazed with murderous hate.

'Someone . . .' it said in its slow deep voice, 'someone . . . is . . . going . . . to . . . die!'

Sir Tumbleweed drew his sword.

'Bags it's you!' he shouted, and with a single

blow he cut through the mighty chain that held up one side of the drawbridge. Neatly as a tightrope-walker he nipped across the top, and with a second swipe he severed the chain on the other side, and jumped clear.

With nothing now to hold it upright, the drawbridge remained for a moment poised above the great green dragon in the moat below. Then, with a tremendous shattering crash, the whole massive, immensely heavy structure came slamming down.

When the echoes of its fall had died away Sir Tumbleweed, peering from his perch, could see no sign of his adversary, save for the tip of its tail which stuck out beneath the far end of the drawbridge.

Feebly the tail-tip twitched, once, twice, three times.

And then it was still.

CHAPTER 13

Sir Tumbleweed scrambled down the gatehouse wall. Still barring his way into the castle was the lowered portcullis, but this was no obstacle to a sword like his. With four strokes he cut an oblong knight-sized hole in it, and stepped through into the courtyard or bailey, ready for any foe. But the place was deserted. Plainly, after raising the drawbridge and dropping the portcullis, the inhabitants had either been eaten (the best people) or had fled. Now the only sound in the empty castle was that cry for help.

Beyond the bailey stood the keep, the strongest part of the fortress, and Sir Tumbleweed could hear that the cry was coming from the topmost turret of the keep. He looked up and saw, in the light of the moon, the flutter of a handkerchief high above.

'Save me! Save me!' called the voice. 'Oh, who will come to my aid?'

'Me!' shouted Sir Tumbleweed. 'Keep calm, fair lady! Do not despair! I'll be with you in half a tick!' And he ran like a stag for the door of the keep. A stout door it was, built to resist the strongest of invaders, but one swipe of the knight's trusty blade sheared through its hinges.

Within was a spiral staircase and up the stone steps he ran, three at a time. He felt supremely happy. At last he had come to the end of his quest. He had won a Tournament, he had defeated a dragon, and in a few moments he would rescue a damsel in distress. And not just any damsel, he felt sure – she would be the girl of his dreams.

He felt like singing *Who is the Most Courageous Knight,* but he refrained, partly because he remembered his promise to Mister Jones, and partly because he was out of breath. Puffing and blowing, Sir Tumbleweed reached the top of the staircase at last. Before him, lit by moonlight streaming in through one of the

turret's windows, was another door. In the upper part of it there was a small grille, through which peered a pair of eyes.

Grey eyes, thought Sir Tumbleweed excitedly, my favourite colour – and she must be tall to be able to see through. I bet everything about her will be just as I imagined, her cheeks, her nose, her mouth, her hair!

'Stand back, fair lady,' he panted. 'I'll have that door down in a jiffy!'

'Save your strength, sir knight,' said a voice within (a low pleasant voice it was, oddly familiar to Sir Tumbleweed's ears), 'save your strength. The door is locked and bolted upon the outer side.'

'How d'you know', said Sir Tumbleweed as he struggled with the great iron key and two heavy bolts, 'that I'm a knight? I wear no armour,' and then the door swung open and the shaft of moonlight flooded the chamber within.

In its glow there stood a figure.

It was dressed all in black. It wore a tall black hat upon its head, and a long black cloak, against whose hem a black cat rubbed itself. A black scarf hid most of its face.

'You!!' gasped the knight.

'Me,' replied the witch.

'But you're not a damsel!'

'Oh yes I am. A damsel is a young unmarried woman. I am not old and I am not wed.'

'But you're not in distress.'

'Oh yes I am. And have been since long before you met me, since my christening in fact.'

'Oh no!' said Sir Tumbleweed. 'Don't tell me it's one of those fairy stories about christenings where there's a wicked godmother who puts a curse on the child?'

'It is,' said the witch, 'and she did. She gave

me a most unwelcome gift.'

'What was it?'

'This,' said the witch.

With one hand she threw aside her tall hat, and with the other she ripped off the black scarf.

Everyone knows what sort of face a witch is supposed to have. Everyone knows about the lank hair and the leathery skin, about the thin lips and the nose that curves to meet the pointed chin.

This face had it all and, try as he would, Sir Tumbleweed could not repress a shudder.

'How do I look?' said the witch drily.

'L-like a witch,' stammered Sir Tumbleweed. There was nothing else he could think of to say.

'Which is what I became, sir knight, when I grew up. There was nothing else I could think of to do. Not with a face like this. So I set myself to learn the arts of witchcraft and the practice of magic.'

'Like vanishing my armour, you mean, and sharpening my sword?'

'That and more. But one thing I could never change.'

'But there's always a good godmother in those stories,' said Sir Tumbleweed, 'whose gift puts everything right.'

'Yes,' said the witch, 'there was. She foretold that one day I would meet a man who would restore the beauty that I would otherwise have had. A good man. A kindly man. A brave man – the bravest of the brave. And I have met him.'

'Me?' said the knight.

'You,' said the witch. 'You, Sir Tumbleweed, Champion of all England, slayer of the great green dragon – you can deliver me from my distress. By one last act of courage. If you will.'

'Of course I will!' cried Sir Tumbleweed. 'What must I do?'

'You must give me something.'

'Anything! Anything at all! What is it that I must give you?'

'A kiss.'

For a long moment there was no sound in the chamber but the purring of Grim the cat as he rubbed himself against the hem of his mistress's cloak.

Sir Tumbleweed's brain whirled. I'd sooner fight a dozen dragons or a hundred knights, he thought wildly, than kiss that frightful ugly mug.

The witch moved a step towards him.

'Faint heart', she said quietly, 'ne'er won fair lady,' and she raised that awful face to his.

'Please,' she said, and in the grey eyes was such a look of pleading, a look that Sir Tumbleweed's knightly courtesy could not withstand.

He shut his eyes tight and, bending forward, aimed a peck at one cheek.

A shudder of disgust ran through him as he felt beneath his lips the leathery skin, but at that instant, the cheek became soft as the skin of a ripe peach.

He stepped back and opened his eyes.

Before him, dressed in a silken gown of forget-me-not blue and a velvet cloak of primrose yellow, with slippers white as snowdrops on her feet, stood a girl. She was not the damsel of his dreams. Her hair was not long and golden and smooth, but short and brown and curly. Her nose was snub, not straight. Her mouth was not a little rosebud, but wide and smiling. And her cheeks were not pale but rosy, as befitted a lady who didn't care two hoots

about the cold winds or the heat of the sun.

Instantly the picture of that cool blonde dream-girl vanished from Sir Tumbleweed's mind, never to return.

'Oh!' he gasped. 'You do look nice! You're as pretty as . . . as a bunch of flowers, as a freshly-picked posy!'

'Shall you call me that?' said she.

'Call you what?'

'Posy. For I must have a name, you know.'

'Posy,' said Sir Tumbleweed. 'Yes. It suits you. The Lady Posy.'

'I should not be that, you know, unless I were to marry a knight.'

Sir Tumbleweed gulped.

'I don't suppose', he said, 'that you would consider marrying a nervous knight, would you, Posy?'

'No, Tummy dear,' said Posy. 'I wouldn't. But I'll certainly marry you.'

CHAPTER 14

Jones the Jet flew in next morning. The sun was shining, the skies were cloudless, and the birds were singing their heads off.

As Taffy circled for his approach, he could see the others far below him on the flat meadow before the castle. While the unicorn grazed near by, the two cats, great Arthur and little Grim, lay side by side watching the knight and his lady.

Tummy and Posy were dancing and, my goodness, how they could dance!

It was no surprise that the lady should be graceful, but no one who had known the old clumsy, gloomy Sir Tumbleweed would have recognized the leaping, laughing figure that twirled and pirouetted on the springy turf.

Taffy Jones gave a final short burn to set himself into his glide-path, and at the sound the dancers stopped and looked up. They could hear him singing as he planed down backwards, and though the Welsh words meant nothing to them, they knew by the lilt of the melody that it was a happy song. In their pleasure at seeing him again, they hardly noticed the pong.

'Taffy!' cried Sir Tumbleweed. 'Great news!'

'Don't tell me, boyo,' said Mister Jones. 'Let me guess. You've killed one of my cousins?'

'Oh crumbs!' said the knight. 'I hadn't thought of it like that.'

'Think no more,' said Taffy, glancing across to the green tail-tip sticking out beneath the end

of the drawbridge. 'I recognize him, see. Stupidest of all the English branch of the family, and that's sayin' somethin'.'

'Anyway, I wasn't going to tell you that,' said Sir Tumbleweed. 'Guess again.'

The red dragon looked at the happy pair standing hand in hand before him, and his huge face split in a grin.

'There's nice!' he said softly. 'There's lovely! Married it is you're goin' to be, or my name's not Taffy Jones.'

And married they were, before the year was many days older.

It was a very quiet wedding, for strangely the attendance was small – perhaps because of the smell of one of the guests.

Posy rode to it on a garlanded Spearhead, and beside her, as she walked up the aisle, was the familiar figure of her lucky black cat. To Sir Tumbleweed, waiting with his best lion at his side, she looked what she was – a dream come true.

And afterwards came the marriage feast (a picnic, they decided, beneath shady trees that bordered a murmuring stream). The change in her looks had robbed Posy of none of her magic powers and, at the snap of her fingers, a great round table appeared laden with choice food.

For the vegetarian Spearhead, there were oats and tender young carrots and fresh clover. For Arthur and Taffy, there were joints of beef and pork and lamb; and for Grim, a dish of fish.

Before the bride and groom, there stood a magnificent wedding-cake which they cut with Sir Tumbleweed's sword, carefully, so as not to damage the decoration on top. This was a miniature castle in icing sugar, perfect in every detail, even to the tiny white handkerchief sticking out of the turret window.

And there were two fine crystal stoups of golden wine for the knight and his lady to drink each other's health; yet as they drank, strangely, the level of the liquid in each glass did not fall but beaded bubbles winked always at the brim.

'What a day, my Lady Posy!' sighed Sir Tumbleweed, as the evening shadows began to fall.

'What a day, my lord!' said his wife.

They sat holding hands, watching the sun go down, while around the table their full-fed friends lay, silently sleeping now.

'What good companions they have been,' said Sir Tumbleweed. 'If we have a son some day, I think it would be nice to name him after one of them.'

'You could hardly call a boy Spearhead,' said Posy.

'Or Grim!'

'Or Taffy!'

'Arthur is a good name though, don't you think, Posy? A noble-sounding name. After all, with a mother like you, a son of ours couldn't fail to become a great man.'

His grey-eyed wife looked fondly at her once nervous knight, with his bright red hair and his long red moustache that now curled so proudly upward.

'With a father like you, Tummy,' she said, 'he might become the greatest of all the knights. Why, he might even become a king.'

Sir Tumbleweed choked on his bubbly wine.

'King Arthur!' he spluttered. 'Don't make me laugh!' And then he did, very long and loudly, so that the lion and the cat and the dragon and the unicorn all woke up.

Jones the Jet yawned hugely.

'What's eatin' you, boyo?' he said.

'Nothing,' said Sir Tumbleweed happily. 'Nothing, I'm glad to say. And talking of eating, why don't we finish off the cake?'

So they did.